Going on a Field Trip

by C.L. Reid
illustrated by Elena Aiello

PICTURE WINDOW BOOKS
a capstone imprint

Emma Every Day is published by
Picture Window Books, an imprint of Capstone
1710 Roe Crest Drive, North Mankato, Minnesota 56003
www.capstonepub.com

Library of Congress Cataloging-in-Publication Data
Names: Reid, C.L., author. | Aiello, Elena (Illustrator), illustrator.
Title: Going on a field trip / by C.L. Reid ; illustrated by Elena Aiello.
Description: North Mankato, MN : Picture Window Books, a Capstone imprint, 2020. | Series: Emma every day | Audience: Ages 5-7. |

Summary: Emma and her third grade class are going on a field trip to the American History Museum and must write about an exhibit they enjoyed; her best friend, Izzie, likes the first ladies' gowns, but Emma decides that her favorite was the portraits of the presidents. Includes an ASL fingerspelling chart, glossary, and content-related questions.

Identifiers: LCCN 2020001362 (print) | LCCN 2020001363 (ebook) |
ISBN 9781515871835 (hardcover) | ISBN 9781515873143 (paperback) |
ISBN 9781515871910 (adobe pdf)

Subjects: LCSH: Deaf children—Juvenile fiction. | Historical museums—Juvenile fiction. | School field trips—Juvenile fiction. | Friendship—Juvenile fiction. | CYAC: Deaf—Fiction. | People with disabilities—Fiction. | National Museum of American History (U.S.)—Fiction. | School field trips—Fiction. | Friendship—Fiction.

Classification: LCC PZ7.1.R4544 Go 2020 (print) |
LCC PZ7.1.R4544 (ebook) | DDC [E]—dc23
LC record available at https://lccn.loc.gov/2020001362
LC ebook record available at https://lccn.loc.gov/2020001363

Image Credits: Capstone: Margeaux Lucas, 28–29
Design Elements: Shutterstock: achii, Mari C, Mika Besfamilnaya

Designer: Tracy McCabe

Printed in the United States 4878

TABLE OF CONTENTS

MEET
EMMA

EMMA CARTER
Age: 8 Grade: 3
SIBLING
One brother, Jaden
(12 years old)
PARENTS
David and Lucy
BEST FRIEND
Izzie Jackson
PET
a goldfish named Ruby
favorite color: teal
favorite food: tacos
favorite school subject: writing
favorite sport: swimming
hobbies: reading, writing, biking, swimming

FINGERSPELLING GUIDE

MANUAL ALPHABET

MANUAL NUMBERS

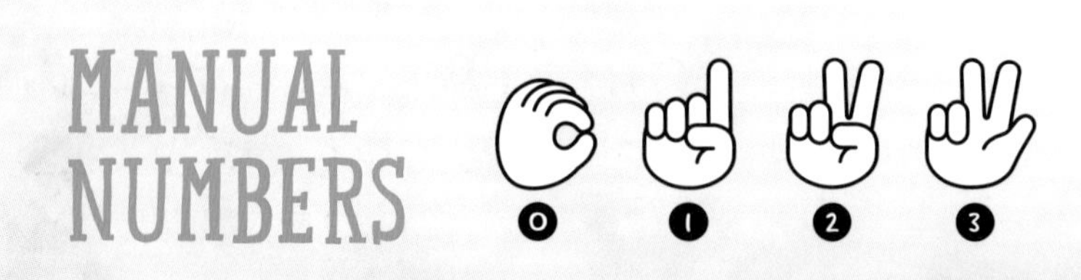

Emma is Deaf. She uses American Sign Language (ASL) to communicate with her family. She also uses a Cochlear Implant (CI) to help her hear.

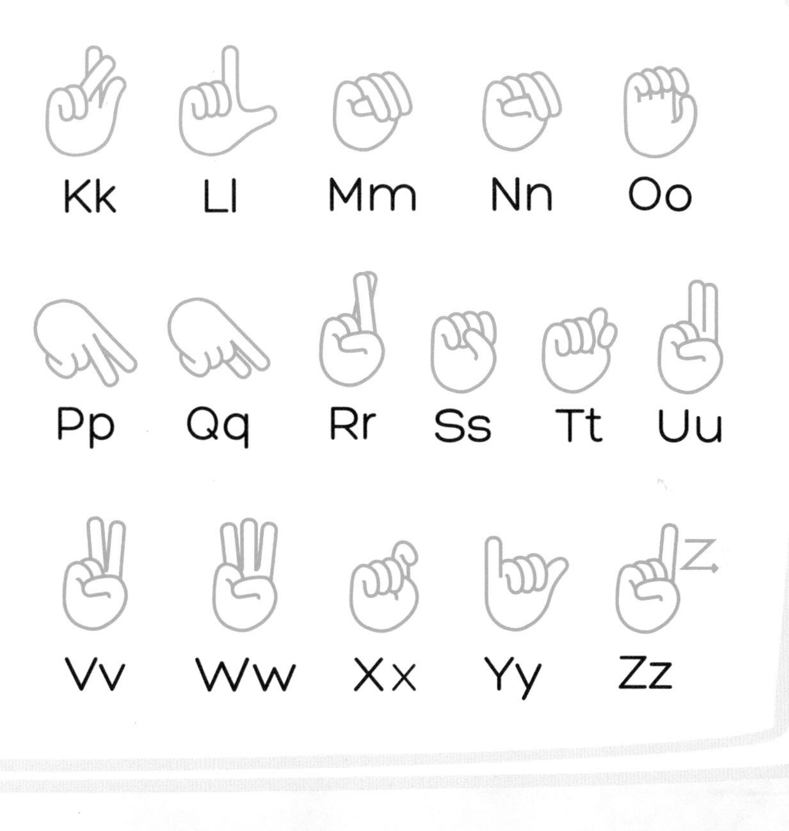

4 5 6 7 8 9 10

Chapter 1

The Helper

For weeks and weeks, Emma had been counting down the days. And today was the big day! It was the class field trip to the American History Museum.

Emma was extra excited because she loved history.

After a short but bumpy ride, the class made it to the museum. The teacher stood and started to talk.

Emma heard Mrs. Buckley's voice with her Cochlear Implant (CI), but she couldn't make out the words.

Her classroom interpreter was there. Miss Carla signed so Emma would understand.

"Mrs. Buckley says she wants everyone to study the exhibits and write about the one you like best. It is due on Monday," Miss Carla signed.

Mrs. Buckley divided the class into groups of four. Emma was with Izzie, Paul, and Zahra. Miss Carla was their group leader.

Paul tapped Emma's shoulder.

"Can you hear me?" he asked.

“You know I can, Paul,” Emma said, signing and smiling.

“Then why do you need an interpreter?” he asked.

“I can’t always understand all the words, especially when it’s loud,” Emma said, continuing to sign as well.

“Well it will be quiet in the museum,” Paul said. “Quiet and boring.”

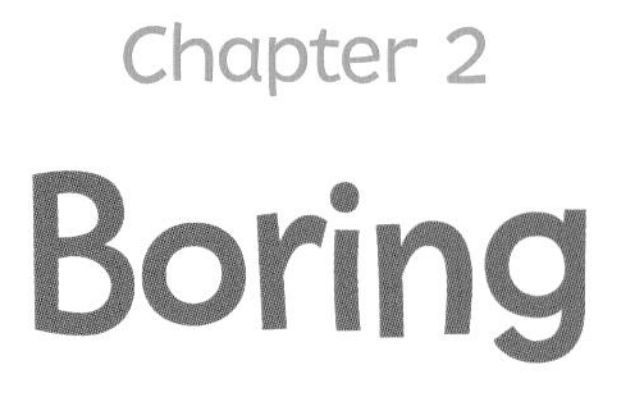

Chapter 2

Boring

Paul was right. It was really quiet inside the museum. But Emma didn't think it was boring. A stagecoach stood near the main entrance. The group stopped to study it.

"Boring," Paul said. "It doesn't even have a radio."

"But it has horses," Zahra said.

"And it's fancy," Izzie said.

"I think it's cool," Emma said.

Miss Carla took them to the next exhibit.

"This flag is from 1812. It inspired Francis Scott Key to write our national anthem," she said and signed.

"Boring," Paul said. "It's just an old flag."

"But it is historic," Zahra said.

"And really important," Izzie said.

"It's amazing that a flag could inspire a song," Emma said.

Next they went to a collection of gowns worn by the first ladies of the United States.

"Boring," Paul said. "How could they even walk through doorways wearing those things?"

"Very carefully," Zahra said.

"It was the style in the old days," Izzie said.

"Wow! I think they are beautiful," Emma said.

In another hallway, the wall was lined with portraits of all the American presidents.

"I'm going to be president when I grow up," Paul said. "My picture will be on this wall too."

"So this isn't so boring?" Emma asked.

"I guess it's not so bad," Paul said.

Chapter 3

President

Emma and her group sat together at lunch. The cafeteria was very loud.

"What was your favorite part of the museum?" Miss Carla asked and signed.

"Lunch," Paul said, making everyone laugh. "I actually liked the presidents' portraits best."

"I liked the first ladies' gowns and the flag," Izzie signed.

"I really liked the stagecoach," Zahra said.

“I liked the presidents’ portraits,” Emma said.

“Maybe we can both be president some day,” Paul said.

“Maybe you can be my vice president,” Emma said.

“Or you can be mine,” Paul said.

After lunch it was time to head back to school. The kids got on the bus and talked the whole way back.

That night Emma told her pet fish, Ruby, all about her day. Then she started on her homework.

"I liked the presidents' portraits. They helped me understand that the United States is very old. There is a lot of history to learn," she wrote.

She kept writing. "If I'm not president when I grow up, I want to work in a museum. Then I can study history every day."

Emma finished her homework, climbed into bed, and dreamed of her future.

LEARN TO SIGN

homework

1. Move hand up cheek.
2. Tap wrists together once.

teacher

1. Move hands away from forehead.
2. Open hands and move them down body.

read

Slide fingers across palm.

book

Open hands like
opening a book.

quiet

Move hands away
from mouth.

history

Make H shape and shake
fingers twice.

GLOSSARY

Cochlear Implant (also called CI)—a device that helps someone who is Deaf to hear; it is worn on the head just above the ear

deaf—being unable to hear

exhibit—a display that usually includes objects and information to show and tell people about a certain subject

fingerspell—to make letters with your hands to spell out words; often used for names of people and places

interpreter—a person who hears one language and translates its meaning to another person

portrait—a drawing, painting, or photograph of a person

sign—use hand gestures to communicate

sign language—a language in which hand gestures, along with facial expressions and body movements, are used instead of speech

stagecoach—a horse-drawn vehicle for carrying people and goods

TALK ABOUT IT

1. If you could go anywhere on a field trip, where would you go? Talk about your answer.
2. Do you think it was fair of the teacher to assign homework after the field trip? Explain your answer.
3. Emma and Paul said they would like to be president. Would you want to be president? Why or why not?

WRITE ABOUT IT

1. Emma loves history. Write about your favorite school subject.
2. What do you want to do when you grow up? Make a list of at least three jobs you would like.
3. Pretend you are Emma. Write a thank-you letter to your teacher for taking you on the field trip.

ABOUT THE AUTHOR

Deaf-blind since childhood, C.L. Reid received a Cochlear Implant (CI) as an adult to help her hear, and she uses American Sign Language (ASL) to communicate. She and her husband have three sons. Their middle son is also deaf-blind. Reid earned a master's degree in writing for children and young adults at Hamline University in St. Paul, Minnesota. Reid lives in Minnesota with her husband, two of their sons, and their cats.

ABOUT THE ILLUSTRATOR

Elena Aiello is an illustrator and character designer. After graduating as a marketing specialist, she decided to study art direction and CGI. Doing so, she discovered a passion for illustration and conceptual art. She works as a freelancer for various magazines and publishers. Aiello loves video games and sushi and lives with her husband and her little pug, Gordon, in Milan, Italy.